THIS BOOK

belongs to

. . . .

For Elodie and Orla, and the adventures that lie ahead. – B.L.

For my Woodbine family, who kept me sane while I couldn't go outside. Love, M.R.

Published in 2022 by Welbeck Editions
An imprint of Welbeck Children's Limited,
part of Welbeck Publishing Group.
Based in London and Sydney.
www.welbeckpublishing.com

Associate Publisher: Laura Knowles
Designer: Deborah Vickers

A CIP catalogue record for this book is available from the British Library.

HB: 978-1-91351-981-0
PB: 978-1-91351-980-3

Printed in Dongguan, China
10 9 8 7 6 5 4 3 2 1

FSC
www.fsc.org
MIX
Paper from
responsible sources
FSC® C144853

let's go OUTSIDE!

Ben Lerwill

Marina Ruiz

W

WELBECK
EDITIONS

Let's go outside!

Let's climb really BIG hills.

Let's be very BRAVE explorers.

Let's feel the wind in our hair.

Let's feel the sun on our faces.

Let's be nature detectives
hunting for minibeasts.

Let's do lots and lots of roly polies!

Let's make the best den
in the whole **w i d e** world.

Let's find a big sploshy puddle to splash in!

Let's wrap up toasty-warm when it's cold.

Let's run as *fast* as our legs can carry us.

Then let's go home and get cosy ...
until it's time for our next adventure!

Now it's time for YOU to go outside!

Nature is full of different colours.
Grass is green, the sky is blue, and
autumn leaves are red.

*What other colourful things do
you see when you play outside?*

Playing outside helps us stay strong. Fresh air
keeps our bodies healthy — and running, climbing
and exploring keeps us fit and happy!

What do you like best about being outside?

Sometimes it's hot and sunny. Sometimes it's cold and snowy. Sometimes it's wet and splashy! It's always important to wear the right clothes for the right weather.

What would you wear on a summer's day?

And what would you wear for a windy walk in the woods?

Being outdoors lets us use all our senses.

What can you SMELL when you're outside?

What can you HEAR?

What can you TOUCH? A hard tree trunk? Squelchy mud? Can you think of other things?

No matter where we live, there's always somewhere to play outside. It might be a park, a playground, a garden, a beach or even a forest!

Where's your favourite place to play?

Outside, birds fly across the sky, bugs wriggle through the earth and furry animals scurry between trees. In different ways, they're all amazing.

What sort of creatures do you like to spot?

How can we help our wildlife?

It's fun to plant things outside and watch them grow. Flowers, vegetables... even trees!

Have you ever planted anything?

What would you most like to grow?

Think of all the different things we can do outside. We can...

...run, dig, build, skip, chase, climb, ride, swing, play, slide, throw, catch, splash, shout, sing, share, find, jump, learn... and lots of other things too!

What else can you think of?